DEALING WITH ADDICTION

VAPING ADDICTION

by Elizabeth Hobbs Voss

BrightPoint Press

San Diego, CA

© 2023 BrightPoint Press
an imprint of ReferencePoint Press, Inc.
Printed in the United States

For more information, contact:
BrightPoint Press
PO Box 27779
San Diego, CA 92198
www.BrightPointPress.com

ALL RIGHTS RESERVED.

No part of this work covered by the copyright hereon may be reproduced or used in any form or by any means—graphic, electronic, or mechanical, including photocopying, recording, taping, web distribution, or information storage retrieval systems—without the written permission of the publisher.

Content Consultant: Michael Joseph Blaha, M.D., M.P.H., Director of Clinical Research, Ciccarone Center for the Prevention of Cardiovascular Disease

LIBRARY OF CONGRESS CATALOGING-IN-PUBLICATION DATA

Names: Voss, Elizabeth Hobbs, author.
Title: Vaping addiction / by Elizabeth Hobbs Voss.
Description: San Diego, CA: BrightPoint Press, [2023] | Series: Dealing with addiction | Includes bibliographical references and index. | Audience: Grades 10-12
Identifiers: LCCN 2022008602 (print) | LCCN 2022008603 (eBook) | ISBN 9781678203825 (hardcover) | ISBN 9781678203832 (eBook)
Subjects: LCSH: Vaping--Juvenile literature. | Nicotine addiction--Juvenile literature.
Classification: LCC RC567 .V67 2023 (print) | LCC RC567 (eBook) | DDC 616.86/5--dc23/eng/20220318
LC record available at https://lccn.loc.gov/2022008602
LC eBook record available at https://lccn.loc.gov/2022008603

CONTENTS

AT A GLANCE   4

INTRODUCTION   6
JESSICA DECIDES TO QUIT VAPING

CHAPTER ONE   12
WHAT IS VAPING ADDICTION?

CHAPTER TWO   22
THE SCIENCE OF VAPING ADDICTION

CHAPTER THREE   30
THE EFFECTS OF VAPING ADDICTION

CHAPTER FOUR   48
TREATING VAPING ADDICTION

Glossary   58
Source Notes   59
For Further Research   60
Index   62
Image Credits   63
About the Author   64

AT A GLANCE

- Vaping is using an e-cigarette. Users breathe in an aerosol, also called a vapor. E-cigarette vapor is a gas. It contains flavoring, nicotine, and other chemicals.

- The minimum legal age for vaping is twenty-one. But teens find ways to get e-cigarettes.

- E-cigarettes are popular with youth. In 2021, 2 million American high school and middle school students vaped.

- E-cigarettes are not safe. Many contain nicotine. This drug is addictive. It can harm the brain.

- E-cigarette vapor contains cancer-causing chemicals.

- Vaping can damage the lungs. It can also hurt the heart.

- Many programs help teens quit vaping. Some are online. Others are in schools.

- Teens get support from quit coaches and therapists. Friends and family also help.

- Doctors help teens quit. They suggest treatment strategies. Sometimes they prescribe drugs.

INTRODUCTION

JESSICA DECIDES TO QUIT VAPING

Jessica first tried vaping at a party. Her friends were doing it. She liked the bubblegum flavor. Then she decided to buy her own e-cigarette. Her older friend bought one for her at the gas station.

She liked vaping while she did her homework. It relaxed her. She also vaped with friends. They talked about maybe trying normal cigarettes too.

Jessica didn't know vaping was bad for her health. She didn't know the vapor contained **nicotine**. After a while, she

It is illegal to sell e-cigarettes to people younger than twenty-one. But many teens still find ways to get vaping supplies.

started coughing often. Jessica had always been a straight-A student. Lately, her grades were slipping.

Her mom was worried. She read about vaping. She learned it wasn't healthy. She urged Jessica to quit. Jessica decided she wanted to quit. She didn't like the coughing.

Jessica looked up vaping online. She learned it could cause **addiction** to nicotine. She read it could change her brain function. It might make it hard to concentrate. Vaping could even hurt her lungs and heart. What Jessica read scared her.

People can use online resources to help them stop vaping.

She found advice about how to quit. Jessica and her friend Stacy decided to quit together. They worked through a program. Each girl had setbacks. But finally, both quit vaping.

E-CIGARETTE EPIDEMIC

Many American teenagers use electronic cigarettes, called e-cigarettes. An e-cigarette heats liquid called **e-juice**. The liquid contains nicotine. It also has flavorings and other chemicals. Heating it creates an **aerosol** that the user breathes. This aerosol is often called a vapor.

E-cigarettes have many shapes and sizes. Some are reusable. Each has a battery and a container for liquid. There is also a mouthpiece. Some look like cigarettes. Others look like flash drives or pens.

E-cigarette use has been growing in popularity among middle and high school students.

E-cigarettes are considered a tobacco product. Most contain the drug nicotine. Nicotine comes from tobacco. It is addictive. Vapers often become addicted to nicotine. Vaping addiction is a major problem among American youth. Experts call it an **epidemic**.

1

WHAT IS VAPING ADDICTION?

People have smoked tobacco for thousands of years. The dried leaves are smoked in cigarettes, cigars, and pipes. Tobacco contains nicotine. Nicotine is highly addictive.

A new way of getting nicotine is vaping. Nicotine is removed from tobacco. It is put in e-juice. Research shows e-cigarettes may be more addictive than cigarettes.

THE HISTORY OF E-CIGARETTES

People began smoking cigarettes in the early 1800s in the United States. Smoking

Nicotine is extracted from tobacco leaves by turning the leaves into a pulp.

was linked to lung cancer and other diseases in the late 1940s. E-cigarettes were invented as a safer alternative.

Herbert A. Gilbert created a smokeless, nontobacco cigarette in 1963. Moist, flavored air replaced burning tobacco. A battery-powered heating device heated the flavor elements. In 2003, a more modern electronic cigarette was made in China.

Cigarette smoking kills about half a million Americans every year. Many measures have curbed smoking. One is anti-tobacco campaigns. Another is smoke-free areas in public places. A third is cigarette taxes. Smoking rates dropped greatly after 1965 in the United States. Forty-three percent of adults smoked in 1965. Only 14 percent smoked in 2019. Among youth, 28 percent smoked in 1991. Three percent did in 2020.

ARE E-CIGARETTES SAFE?

E-cigarettes are safer than cigarettes. But they are not safe. Vapor has fewer chemicals than cigarette smoke. But it still contains harmful chemicals. Vapor contains nicotine and toxic metals. And it has chemicals that cause cancer. Vaping can damage the brain, lungs, and heart. Health experts say no tobacco product is safe.

Cigarette smoking has become less popular. But vaping has grown. Nicotine is addictive. People want to keep using it but don't want to smoke. Vaping is an attractive option. Stores began selling e-cigarettes in the United States in the mid-2000s. Sales rose quickly. Marketing helped. Ads targeted youth. E-cigarette companies put ads on social media.

The ads featured celebrities. E-cigarette companies sponsored concerts and offered scholarships. The companies also created more flavors. These flavors attracted young people to vaping.

TYPES OF E-CIGARETTES

Tanks & Vape Mods

- Larger than other e-cigarettes
- Customizable
- Can be recharged
- Refillable with e-juice

Pod Mod E-cigarettes

- Smaller than tanks and vape mods
- Can be recharged
- Pre-filled or refillable with e-juice

Disposable E-cigarettes

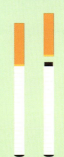

- Only used once and thrown away
- Some are rechargeable
- Cannot be refiled

POPULAR AMONG YOUTH

Vaping is most popular among teens. More teens use e-cigarettes than smoke. In 2019, 28 percent of American high schoolers vaped. In middle schools, 11 percent used e-cigarettes. These numbers worried health experts.

Vaping rates dropped in 2020. They fell again in 2021. The COVID-19 pandemic affected e-cigarette use. Stores were closed. Schools switched to remote learning. It was harder for teens to get e-cigarettes. Laws also made vaping illegal for people under twenty-one. In 2021, only 11 percent of high schoolers vaped. Even so, 2 million teens said they used e-cigarettes. Some experts think that studies may underestimate use.

A vaping culture has grown. Teenagers feel pressure to try e-cigarettes. They think it is cool. Teens have contests. They see who can blow the largest vape rings.

They share e-cigarettes. They vape in

school bathrooms.

Teens like the flavors. These include fruit

and candy. They like the lack of smoke.

TELEVISION SHOWS PRESENT E-CIGARETTES AS COOL

Popular TV shows feature vaping. It may seem attractive and cool. The hit drama *Euphoria* is an example. It shows vaping sixty-seven times in its first season. But actress Barbie Ferreira wants to quit vaping. "I'm actually trying to quit my [e-cigarette] because it's really bad for you," she said.

Quoted in Ernesto Macias, "Barbie Ferreira Is Not Worried About the Future, She's Just Trying to Quit Her Juul," Interview, *August 12, 2019. www.interviewmagazine.com.*

Vaping is cheaper than smoking cigarettes.

Teenagers think it is safer.

TOBACCO COMPANIES FIND NEW PROFITS IN VAPING

"E-cigarettes have the potential to addict a new generation that might not otherwise have experimented with traditional cigarettes," says Patricia Folan.[1] Folan is a registered nurse. She is also director of the Center for Tobacco Control at Northwell Health in New York. Cigarette makers produce vaping products. "Basically, these Big Tobacco corporations are replacing

Kids as young as twelve years old are trying e-cigarettes.

their old cigarette customers with new, younger [e-cigarette] customers," says Folan.²

2
THE SCIENCE OF VAPING ADDICTION

Addiction is a substance use disorder (SUD). Those with SUD use a drug despite its harmful consequences. They have a strong focus on using the drug. Their ability to function in daily life is upset.

People with SUD have distorted thinking. Brain imaging shows changes in the brain.

These changes are in areas responsible for judgment, decision making, learning, memory, and behavioral control.

Nicotine is absorbed into the blood when someone vapes. This affects the brain in

Nicotine can damage the prefrontal cortex of adolescent brains. The prefrontal cortex controls emotions and impulses.

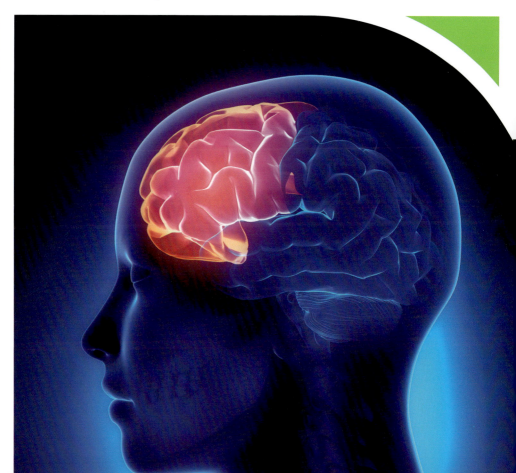

ten seconds. The brain is flooded with the chemical messenger dopamine. Dopamine makes a person feel good. It brings positive feelings. These feelings include relaxation and focus. Vapers also feel calm and happy. But these feelings do not last.

Nicotine leaves the body soon after entering. The vaper wants another puff almost right away. This causes a vicious cycle of addiction. "Nicotine, alcohol, heroin, or any drug of abuse works by hijacking the brain's reward system," says Nii Addy.[3] Addy is a Yale researcher. He specializes in the brain science of addiction.

E-CIGARETTES MAY BE MORE ADDICTIVE THAN CIGARETTES

A study compared nicotine dependence in young cigarette smokers and e-cigarette users. The e-cigarette users were twice as addicted to nicotine. The study suggests that e-cigarettes may be more addictive than cigarettes.

CRAVINGS AND TRIGGERS

Addicted users crave e-cigarettes. They want to vape with friends. They crave e-cigarettes when they study or watch TV. They want the good feelings that dopamine provides. Emotions can make users vape. These emotions include anxiety and

Being around others who are vaping can trigger nicotine cravings.

boredom. Even happiness can make users crave e-cigarettes.

Triggers also make addicted users want to vape. Triggers are situations or activities that remind a user of vaping. Some triggers are social. Going to a party or hanging out with friends might be triggers. Everyday activities like doing homework or driving can be triggers too. Triggers can change the amount of dopamine in the brain. This unleashes intense cravings. Cravings make it hard for addicted users to quit nicotine.

WITHDRAWAL SYMPTOMS

Vapers often become addicted to nicotine. Over time, they need more nicotine to get the same effect. This is called tolerance. It is difficult for people with vaping addiction to stop. They may continue to vape despite health problems. Trying to quit causes **withdrawal**.

Stopping nicotine use is jarring. Less dopamine is released in the brain. This affects the brain's pleasure center. It is responsible for mood and behavior. Withdrawal symptoms result.

CAN VAPING HELP TEENS STOP SMOKING?

Vaping is sometimes marketed as a way to stop smoking cigarettes. But experts do not suggest teens try this. Research shows little evidence that it works. Some teens end up smoking and vaping. Instead, teen smokers can see a doctor or a specialist for help.

Strong cravings come with withdrawal. Emotions are aroused. Some people feel anxious and irritable. Others get angry, stressed, or depressed. Physical symptoms accompany withdrawal. It may be difficult to concentrate. Sitting still may be tough. Some people get especially hungry. Others get constipated. It can be hard to sleep.

Nicotine withdrawal often begins only hours after quitting vaping. Symptoms last a few days to several weeks. They peak on the second or third day. They improve each day after the peak.

3
THE EFFECTS OF VAPING ADDICTION

Vapers may have short-term side effects. Some vapers have dry mouth or a cough. Others may feel dizzy. Their skin and eyes could be dry. Some vapers have nosebleeds.

E-cigarettes are relatively new. The long-term effects of vaping are unknown.

However, evidence suggests it damages the lungs, heart, and brain. Those addicted to vaping risk these long-term effects.

HARM TO THE LUNGS

Vaping irritates the lungs' airways. Some studies suggest that e-cigarette chemicals

Coughing is a common side effect of vaping.

may injure the lungs. Vaping worsens symptoms of COPD. COPD is a serious lung disease. Its main cause is smoking. Vaping may increase the risk of getting COPD. Research has not proven this risk. The illness develops over many years. E-cigarettes haven't been around very long. But some studies suggest there may be a link. More research is needed. "Long gone are the days when makers of e-cigarettes could claim that this form of nicotine use was not harmful," says Dr. Len Horovitz.[4] He is a pulmonary specialist at Lenox Hill Hospital in New York City.

Vaping irritates the airways. The irritation makes asthma attacks more likely.

Vaping may increase the risk of asthma. Asthma is a condition that makes breathing difficult by swelling airways. Vaping worsens symptoms of asthma. E-cigarette vapor contains tiny particles. These are inhaled. They go deep into the lungs. These particles may worsen asthma and COPD.

Linda Richter is vice president for prevention research and analysis at the Partnership to End Addiction. She says that athletes who vape may quickly get out of breath. Vaping can hurt athletes' performance. "I couldn't stay on the ice for more than a minute and a half before being gassed," says Cade Beauparlant. He played hockey in high school. "My lungs couldn't

VAPERS RISK GETTING COVID-19

Teens who vape are more likely to get COVID-19, according to one study. Their risk is five times higher than those who don't vape. Vaping damages their lungs, and COVID-19 affects the lungs. The risk is higher for those who smoke too. Their risk is seven times higher.

handle it. I felt like I couldn't pull enough air into my lungs."[5]

HARM TO THE HEART

Nicotine may stiffen arteries. Arteries are blood vessels. They carry blood away from the heart. Nicotine may also cause blood clots. It raises blood pressure and spikes adrenaline. Adrenaline is a chemical the body releases. It makes the heart beat faster.

All of these effects increase the possibility of heart attack and stroke. Vaping every day doubles the risk of a person having a heart

Using e-cigarettes daily may double a person's chances of having a heart attack.

attack. Nicotine from either e-cigarettes or traditional cigarettes can contribute to this risk.

HARM TO YOUNG BRAINS

Nicotine harms growing brains. It can damage the prefrontal cortex. This part of the brain develops until age twenty-five. It is responsible for emotional control, decision-making, and impulse control. Vapers may have trouble concentrating. It could be tough to pay attention in class.

Youth who vape are at risk for developing mood disorders. They are more likely to suffer from depression and anxiety. They may have lower impulse control. Vaping is particularly bad for teenagers with ADHD. ADHD is a disorder that makes it difficult for people to pay attention and sit still. Vapers with ADHD like the increased focus they experience at first. But ultimately, vaping worsens their symptoms. They become nervous and anxious.

PATH TO OTHER DRUG USE

Teens become addicted to nicotine more easily than adults. Nicotine primes them to become addicted to other drugs. It changes the structure of DNA. It reprograms genes that are related to addiction.

Vaping may lead to smoking. Research has shown that youth who have vaped

In one study, e-cigarettes were found to be likely responsible for nearly 200,000 new cigarette users.

are seven times more likely to smoke later. One study says e-cigarettes are likely responsible for 15 percent of current cigarette use among teens.

DANGEROUS CHEMICALS

E-cigarette vapor contains many harmful chemicals. Some vape flavorings have diacetyl. It may be dangerous to inhale. It has been linked to popcorn lung. This illness damages the lungs' smallest airways.

The United Kingdom banned diacetyl from e-cigarettes. However, it remains in e-juice sold in the United States. The American Lung Association wants diacetyl banned from e-cigarettes. So far, no vapers have gotten popcorn lung. More research is needed to understand the effects of diacetyl.

E-cigarette vapor contains traces of nearly 2,000 unknown chemicals. Scientists don't know the effects of these chemicals.

Vapor also contains benzene. This is a pollutant in city air. Benzene is tied to leukemia. This type of cancer affects white blood cells. E-cigarette vapor contains many other chemicals and metals. Some cause cancer. These **carcinogens** include

Severe cases of EVALI require mechanical ventilation to help people breathe.

arsenic and lead. The effect of the amounts of carcinogens in e-cigarettes is unknown.

LUNG INJURIES OUTBREAK

In the summer of 2019, sickness broke out in the United States. A total of 2,807 people were hospitalized. Sixty-eight people died.

They had EVALI. This is a sudden lung illness from vaping.

Patients had fevers. Their hearts beat fast. Their chests hurt. Breathing was hard. They coughed, vomited, and had diarrhea. They were given oxygen. Nearly a third of patients went on ventilators. Ventilators are devices that help people breathe.

Most patients had used products containing THC. THC is found in cannabis. It makes people high. Vitamin E acetate was in patients' lungs. This chemical is an artificial form of vitamin E. It is added to some products that contain THC. Vitamin E acetate is dangerous to inhale. It may interfere with normal lung function.

EVALI cases peaked in September 2019. Then they dropped gradually. Some states have banned vitamin E acetate from vaping products. But it remains in illegal products. Health officials urge vapers to avoid

THE FDA

The Food and Drug Administration (FDA) is a federal agency that makes sure drugs are safe and effective. It stops factories from making banned e-cigarettes. The FDA also works with Scholastic. Scholastic is an educational publisher. It creates learning materials. The learning materials teach teens about the dangers of tobacco products, including e-cigarettes.

products with THC. Also, users should buy e-cigarettes only from licensed sellers.

VAPING AND COMMUNITIES

Many people are trying to curb youth vaping. In 2020, a federal law made teen vaping illegal. The lowest legal age for it became twenty-one. Nevertheless, teens found ways to keep vaping illegally.

In 2020, a federal law banned some types of e-cigarettes. The law was meant to reduce youth vaping. Stores can no longer sell products that use flavored **pods**. Flavoring helps lead to addiction. One brand

Prefilled pods came in flavors such as mango.

called Juul used these pods. Juul was very popular with teens.

But the law has many gaps. It disallows only flavored pods. Many vape products, such as tanks, mods, and disposable e-cigarettes, do not use pods. They still have flavors. Also, newer e-cigarettes are not banned.

States have laws about vaping. Some restrict sales of flavored e-cigarettes. Some impose e-cigarette taxes. Others require licenses to sell e-cigarettes. Many have laws about packaging. For instance, laws require e-juice to be sold in child-resistant bottles.

Smoke-free laws ban smoking in public places. Twenty-eight states and the District of Columbia have these laws. They protect people from secondhand smoke. As of 2020, sixteen states and the District of Columbia added e-cigarettes to these laws. Many cities and towns ban vaping in public places.

4

TREATING VAPING ADDICTION

Many programs help teens quit vaping. Teens learn about the dangers of vaping and how to quit in school. The American Lung Association and the Truth Initiative have lesson plans for youth. Smokefree Teen is a website run by the National Cancer Institute. The website's goal is to reduce the number of youth who use tobacco products. Teens can make quit plans online. First, they pick a quit date. Then they think about how vaping hurts them. It may harm their health. Some think it is too expensive. Vaping can cost between

Supportive friends, family, and professionals help people quit vaping.

$1,000 and $1,500 a year. The vapers

decide why they want to quit and consider

why they vape. They plan on how to deal

with cravings. Finally, they find support.

SUPPORT IS KEY TO QUITTING

Smokefree Teen suggests teens find a

support person. It could be a friend. It might

HOW TO HANDLE CRAVINGS

Cravings come when people try to quit vaping. Many strategies help ease cravings. One strategy is distraction. Distractions can include playing games, exercising, or watching TV. Another strategy is to think about the reasons for quitting. A third strategy is to talk with someone who supports quitting.

be parents or another trusted adult. It could also be a quit coach.

Quit coaches are trained volunteers. They help teens quit. They give them tips about dealing with cravings. They talk about withdrawal symptoms. The Centers for Disease Control and Prevention is a US federal agency. It has free quit coaches. Some states have help lines.

My Life, My Quit is a website. It helps teens quit tobacco products. Teens get text, phone, and online support. The program is run by National Jewish Health. Supportive counseling also helps. Therapists build

a trusting relationship with patients.
They provide support, resources, and
judgment-free guidance.

TEXT MESSAGE PROGRAMS AND SOCIAL MEDIA

Text message programs are another helpful
tool. This Is Quitting is one program run
by the Truth Initiative. The program is free
to join. Teens text "DITCHVAPE" to the
program's number. The program sends
them texts. One example text says, "I'm not
here to judge or make you feel bad—even if
you slip after you quit. I'll also share quitting

Text message programs effectively help teens quit vaping.

tips from others like you who have quit or are trying, too."[6]

Social media can also help teens quit vaping. TikTok creators, called influencers, use This Is Quitting. Then they talk about the experience on TikTok. Influencer Victoria Annunziato says, "I'm hopeful that my journey will inspire others and spread awareness."[7] The TikTok influencers invite young people to join them and quit together.

HOW TO MANAGE NICOTINE WITHDRAWAL

Nicotine withdrawal varies from person to person. It can make quitting difficult. But it eases up as time passes. Eating healthy snacks, drinking plenty of water, exercising, and getting enough sleep all help with the symptoms. People may also get support from family and friends. Making a quit plan can help people think long-term. People trying to quit can make a plan at Smokefree.gov.

On YouTube, teens share their quitting stories on *Quitters*. The first episode is called "How a 3 Year Vaper Quit Vaping in 4 Days."

HELP FROM A DOCTOR

Doctors may prescribe nicotine replacement therapy (NRT). NRT helps people stop using tobacco products. Nicotine patches are often part of the treatment. The patches provide low doses of nicotine. This reduces cravings and withdrawal symptoms.

Doctors may prescribe drugs if NRT fails. Two examples are bupropion and varenicline. Both are approved by the Food and Drug Administration. Health care providers can also help patients who have developed physical problems. These problems may include breathing troubles or difficulty concentrating.

ENDING THE VAPING EPIDEMIC

Vaping addiction is a major problem affecting American youth. Research suggests e-cigarettes damage the lungs, brain, and heart. This jeopardizes the health of a large proportion of youth. Fortunately, growing awareness has led to widespread

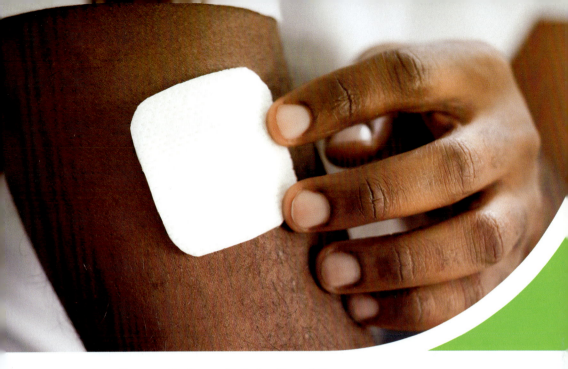

Nicotine patches stick to the skin.

efforts. Teens are educated about vaping in schools and online. Federal, state, and local laws help curb youth vaping. Many programs in schools, online, and on social media help teens quit vaping. The prospects are good for ending the epidemic of youth vaping.

GLOSSARY

addiction
a strong and harmful need to regularly have or do something

aerosol
liquid or solid particles suspended in a gas

carcinogens
substances that cause cancer

e-juice
the liquid used in e-cigarettes to create vapor

epidemic
a sudden, quickly spreading occurrence of something harmful or unwanted

nicotine
a poisonous material in tobacco that addicts people to tobacco products

pods
small plastic containers that hold e-juice

withdrawal
physical and mental symptoms that happen after stopping or reducing intake of a drug

SOURCE NOTES

CHAPTER ONE: WHAT IS VAPING ADDICTION?

1. Patricia Folan, "The Truth About Vaping," *Northwell Health*, May 10, 2018. www.northwell.edu.

2. Folan, "The Truth About Vaping."

CHAPTER TWO: THE SCIENCE OF VAPING ADDICTION

3. Quoted in Jomo Kwame Sundaram and Wan Manan Muda, "Vaping Fad Boosts Dangerous Nicotine Addiction," *Global Issues*, September 10, 2019. www.globalissues.org.

CHAPTER THREE: THE EFFECTS OF VAPING ADDICTION

4. "More Studies Link Vaping to Asthma, COPD," *Thompson Health*, January 14, 2020. www.thompsonhealth.com.

5. Quoted in Erika Edwards, "Vaping Is Hurting Teenage Athletes, Dashing Their Future in Sports," *NBC News*, July 10, 2019. www.nbcnews.com.

CHAPTER FOUR: TREATING VAPING ADDICTION

6. Quoted in "Quitting E-cigarettes," *Truth Initiative*, January 19, 2019. https://truthinitiative.org.

7. Quoted in "First-of-Its-Kind truth® Campaign Follows Young Vapers Quit E-cigarettes Live on Social Media," *Truth Initiative*, January 26, 2021. https://truthinitiative.org.

FOR FURTHER RESEARCH

BOOKS

Sherri Mabry Gordon, *Everything You Need to Know About Smoking, Vaping, and Your Health*. New York: Rosen Young Adult, 2019.

Lisa Idzikowski, *The Dangers of Vaping*. New York: Power Kids Press, 2020.

Sheila Llanas, *Drug and Alcohol Addiction.* San Diego, CA: BrightPoint Press, 2023.

INTERNET SOURCES

"How a 3 Year Vaper Quit Vaping in 4 Days: Quitters Episode 1," *YouTube*, uploaded by truthorange, March 12, 2021. www.youtube.com.

"Quick Facts on the Risks of E-cigarettes for Kids, Teens, and Young Adults," *Centers for Disease Control and Prevention*, n.d. www.cdc.gov.

Janet Raloff, "These Free Programs Can Help Teens Seeking to Quit Vaping," *Science News for Students*, October 27, 2020. www.sciencenewsforstudents.org.

WEBSITES

My Life, My Quit
www.mylifemyquit.com

This is a website for teens who want to quit using tobacco products, including e-cigarettes. It is run by National Jewish Health. It features teens talking about their experiences. It provides information and tools to help teens quit.

Smokefree Teen
https://teen.smokefree.gov

Smokefree Teen helps teens stop using tobacco products such as e-cigarettes. Smokefree Teen is part of the National Cancer Institute's Smokefree.gov initiative.

Truth Initiative
https://truthinitiative.org

Truth Initiative is a nonprofit health organization. It is committed to ending tobacco use and nicotine addiction. The website has many articles about vaping and tools teens can use to quit vaping.

INDEX

ADHD, 37–38
American Lung Association, 40, 48
asthma, 33

brain, 8, 15, 22–24, 27–28, 31,
  37–38, 56

cancer, 14, 15, 41, 48
Centers for Disease Control and
  Prevention, 51
chemicals, 10, 15, 24, 31–32, 35,
  40–42, 43–44
COPD, 32–33
coughing, 8, 30, 43
COVID-19, 18, 34
cravings, 25–27, 29, 50, 51, 55

dopamine, 24–25, 27–28

e-juice, 10, 13, 17, 40, 47
EVALI, 42–44

flavors, 6, 10, 14, 16, 19, 40, 45–47
Food and Drug Administration
  (FDA), 44, 56

heart, 8, 15, 31, 35–36, 43, 56

law, 18, 45–47, 57
lungs, 8, 14, 15, 31–35, 40, 42–44,
  48, 56

My Life, My Quit, 51

nicotine, 7, 8, 10–11, 12, 15, 16,
  23–25, 27–29, 32, 35–38, 54, 55
nicotine replacement therapy
  (NRT), 55–56

popcorn lung, 40

quitting, 8–9, 19, 27–29, 48–57

Smokefree Teen, 48, 50
smoking, 12–17, 19–20, 25, 28, 32,
  34, 38–39, 47
substance use disorder (SUD),
  22–23

text message programs, 51, 52–54
tobacco, 11, 12, 14, 15, 20, 44, 49,
  51, 55
triggers, 26–27
Truth Initiative, 48, 52
types of e-cigarettes, 10, 17, 45–46

vapor, 7, 10, 15, 33, 40–41

withdrawal, 27–29, 51, 54, 55

youth, 10–11, 15, 16–21, 25, 28, 34,
  37–39, 44, 45–46, 48–51, 53–55,
  56–57

IMAGE CREDITS

Cover: © Aleksandr Yu/Shutterstock Images
5: © Milan Maksovic/iStockphoto
7: © Eldar Nurkovic/Shutterstock Images
9: © Fizkes/Shutterstock Images
11: © Aleksandr Yu/Shutterstock Images
13: © Zbigniew Guzowski/Shutterstock Images
17 tanks and vapes: © Alexandr III/Shutterstock Images
17 disposable e-cigarettes: © Alexandr III/Shutterstock Images
17 pod mod e-cigarettes: © Anna Gudimova/iStockphoto
21: © Diego Cervo/Shutterstock Images
23: © Cliparea Custom Media/Shutterstock Images
26: © Yuri Arcurs/iStockphoto
31: © Noody/Shutterstock Images
33: © People Images/iStockphoto
36: © Chajamp/Shutterstock Images
39: © Highway Starz Photography/iStockphoto
41: © Ridvan Celik/iStockphoto
42: © Ines Nepo/Shutterstock Images
46: © GG 5795/Shutterstock Images
49: © VH Studio/Shutterstock Images
53: © Marco Piunti/iStockphoto
57: © Andrey Popov/Shutterstock Images

ABOUT THE AUTHOR

Elizabeth Hobbs Voss is a children's author and journalist. She enjoys writing about subjects that matter to young people. She aspires to make a difference in her readers' lives. With this book, she hopes to help teens quit or never start vaping. She lives in New York City with her husband, Todd.